Illustrations copyright © 1984, Takeshi Matsumoto
English edition rights arranged by Kurita-Bando Literary Agency.
English text copyright © 1983, Neugebauer Press Salzburg–London–Boston.
Published by Picture Book Studio, an imprint of Neugebauer Press.
Distributed in USA by Alphabet Press, Natick, MA.
Distributed in Canada by Vanwell Publishing, St. Catharines.
Distributed in G.B. by Ragged Bears, Andover, England.
All rights reserved.
Printed in Austria.

ISBN 0-907234-26-7

Ask your bookseller for these other PICTURE BOOK STUDIO books
illustrated by Chihiro Iwasaki:
THE LITTLE MERMAID by Hans Christian Andersen
SNOW WHITE AND THE SEVEN DWARVES by The Brothers Grimm
THE WISE QUEEN a Folktale
SWANLAKE retold by Anthea Bell.

Hans Christian Andersen
illustrated by Chihiro Iwasaki
translated by Anthea Bell

The Red Shoes

PICTURE BOOK STUDIO

Once upon a time there was a little girl, very pretty and delicate.
She had to go barefoot all summer, because she was poor, and in winter she
wore big wooden clogs which made her little ankles red and sore.
There was an old cobbler woman who lived in the middle of the village. She
sat and sewed a pair of little shoes as best she might, out of scraps of old red
cloth. The shoes were clumsy, but still, the old woman meant well when she
made them for the little girl. The girl's name was Karen.

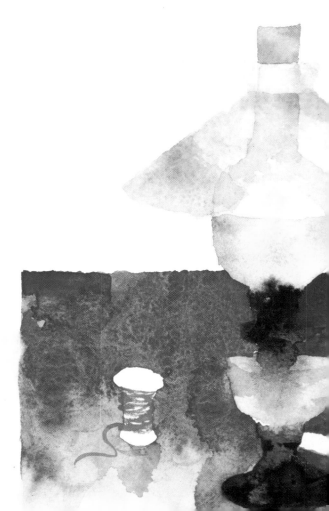

She got the red shoes and wore them for the first time on the very day of her mother's funeral. They were not the right kind of shoes to wear as mourning, but she had no others, so she put the red shoes on her bare feet and wore them as she followed the poor coffin.

Then a big, old-fashioned carriage suddenly came driving by, with a rich old lady sitting in it. The old lady looked at the little girl and felt sorry for her. "Listen," she said to the pastor, "give me that little girl, and I'll look after her well!"

Karen thought she had the red shoes to thank for her good fortune, but the old lady said they were dreadful, and she had them burnt. As for Karen, she was given fine, neat clothes to wear, and she had lessons and learned to sew. People said she was pretty, but her mirror told her, "You are better than pretty, you're beautiful!"

Then, one day, the Queen came travelling through the country, and her little daughter the Princess was with her. People came flocking to stand outside the castle, and Karen was among them. The little Princess stood on a balcony so that they could see her, dressed in white. She had no train or golden crown, but she was wearing beautiful red shoes made of morocco leather, very much finer than the pair the old cobbler woman had made for little Karen. There was nothing like those red shoes in all the world!

By now Karen was old enough to be confirmed. She had new clothes, and she
was to get new shoes too. The rich shoemaker in town measured her feet for
the shoes; he measured them at his house, in his own room, where there were
big glass-fronted cupboards standing around, full of beautiful shoes and
shiny leather boots.

It was all very fine, but sad to say, the old lady could not see very well, so
the sight gave her no pleasure. Among those shoes there was a red pair, just
like the pair the Princess had been wearing. How pretty they were! The
shoemaker said they had been made for a count's daughter, but they did
not fit her.

"They must be made of patent leather!" said the old lady. "How they shine!"
"Oh, yes, they do shine!" said Karen. The shoes fitted her, and they were bought.
However, the old lady did not know they were red. If she had known,
she would never have let Karen go to her confirmation wearing red shoes,
but that was what Karen did. Everyone looked at her feet as she came
into the church and walked up towards the choir. She felt as if even the
old pictures on the tombstones, showing pastors and their wives in
starched ruffs and long black robes, were looking at her red shoes.
She was thinking of nothing else when the pastor laid his hand on her
head and spoke of holy baptism and her covenant with God, and told
her that she must act like a grown Christian woman now. The organ
played solemn music, the children sang, and the old choirmaster sang too,
but all the time Karen was thinking of her red shoes.
That afternoon everyone told the old lady that the shoes Karen was wearing
were red, and the old lady thought that was very wrong and improper.
When Karen went to church in the future, she was always to wear black shoes,
even if they were old ones.

Next Sunday the children who had been confirmed went to their first communion. First Karen looked at the black shoes, and then she looked at the red shoes — and then she looked at the red shoes again, and she put them on. It was beautiful, sunny weather, and Karen and the old lady walked along the footpath through the cornfields. The path was rather dusty.
There was an old soldier standing at the church door. He had a crutch and a curious long beard, more red than white — in fact, it really was red. He bowed very low and asked the old lady if she would like him to dust her shoes. Karen put out her own little foot too. "Why, what pretty dancing-shoes!" said the soldier. "Shoes, fit well when you dance!" And he touched their soles with his hand.

The old lady gave the soldier a coin, and then she went into church with Karen. Everyone inside the church was looking at Karen's red shoes, and all the pictures were looking at them, and when Karen knelt down at the altar and put the golden chalice to her lips, she could think of nothing but the red shoes. It was as if they were floating before her in the chalice, and she forgot to sing the hymn, she forgot to say the Lord's Prayer.

Then all the people came out of church, and the old lady got into her carriage. Karen was raising her foot to step up after her when the old soldier, standing near them, said, "Why, what pretty dancing-shoes!" And Karen could not help dancing a step or two. But once she began, her legs went on dancing and would not stop, as if the shoes had some power over them.

She danced around the corner of the church, for still she could not stop. The coachman had to run after her and catch hold of her. He lifted her up into the carriage, but even there her feet went on dancing, so that she kicked the good old lady. They would not be still until she took the shoes off.

When they got home the shoes were put away in a cupboard, but Karen could not help going to look at them now and then.

Now one day the old lady fell ill, and it was said she was near death. She needed care and nursing all the time, and there was no one more closely related to her than Karen. But there was a great ball in the town, and Karen had been invited. She looked at the old lady, who was sure to die in any case, she looked at the red shoes, and she thought it would be no sin. So she put the red shoes on, and there was no harm in that—but then she went to the ball and began to dance, as she ought not to have done.

However, when she wanted to turn right, the shoes danced left, and when she wanted to go up the ballroom the shoes danced away and down the stairs, along the street and out to the town gate. Dance she did and dance she must, out into the dark wood. She saw a light among the trees and thought it was the moon, for it had a face, but it was the old soldier with the red beard. He sat there nodding, and said, "Why, what pretty dancing-shoes!" Then she was afraid, and she tried to take the red shoes off, but they stuck fast. She tore off her stockings, but the shoes had grown to her feet, and dance she did and dance she must, over meadows and fields, in rain and shine, by day and by night, but it was worst at night.

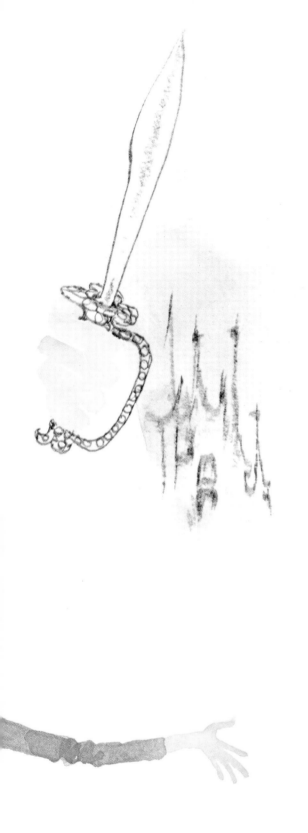

She danced into the churchyard, but the dead at rest there did not dance; they had better things to do. She wanted to sit on the poor man's grave where bitter tansy grew, but there was no rest or peace for her, and when she danced towards the open door of the church, she saw an angel in long white robes, with wings reaching down from his shoulders to the ground. His face was stern and solemn, and he held a broad, shining sword in his hand.

"You shall dance!" he said. "You shall dance in your red shoes until you are pale and cold and nothing but skin and bone. You shall dance from door to door, and wherever proud, vain children live you must knock, so that they will hear you and be afraid! You shall dance and dance..."

"Have mercy!" cried Karen. But she did not hear what the angel said in reply, for the shoes were carrying her through the gateway and out into the fields, over hill and over dale, and still she had to dance.

One morning she danced past a door that she knew
very well. She heard people singing hymns inside, and
a coffin covered with flowers was carried out. Then she
knew the old lady had died, and she felt as if everyone had
abandoned her, and she was cursed by the angel of God.
Dance she did and dance she must, through the dark
night. Her shoes carried her over thorns and briars, and
she was hurt and bleeding. She danced over the heath to a
lonely little house.

It was here, she knew, that the executioner lived, and she
knocked on the window panes and called, "Come out!
Come out! I cannot come in, because I must dance!"
"You can't know who I am!" said the executioner. "I cut off
wicked people's heads, and now I can feel my axe
quivering!"
"Don't cut off my head," said Karen, "for if you do I cannot
repent of my sin! But cut off my feet, with the red shoes on
them."
Then she confessed her grievous sin, and the executioner
cut off her feet with the red shoes. As for the shoes,
however, they danced away over the fields into the deep
wood, with her little feet inside them. The executioner made
her wooden feet and crutches, and taught her a penitential
psalm that poor sinners used to sing, and she kissed the
hand that had held the axe and went on over the heath.

"I have suffered enough for the sake of the red shoes now!" she said. "Now I will go to church, so the people can see me!" She went to the church door as fast as she could go, but when she came near it the red shoes were dancing ahead of her, and she was afraid and turned back.

All week she was sad, and wept bitterly, but when Sunday came she said, "Surely I've suffered and struggled enough now! I should think I am as good as many of the proud people sitting there in church." So she boldly went towards the church, but she had only reached the churchyard gate when suddenly she saw the red shoes dancing ahead of her again. She was afraid, and turned back, repenting of her sin with all her heart.

She went to the parsonage and offered to be a maidservant
there, promising to work hard and do everything she
could. She said she did not want any wages, only to have a
roof over her head again and live with good people. The
pastor's wife felt sorry for her and took her into service. She
worked very hard and was grateful, and she sat listening
quietly when the pastor read aloud from the Bible in the
evenings. The children all loved her, but whenever they
talked about pretty clothes and finery, and said it must be
lovely to look like a queen, Karen shook her head.
When Sunday came they all went to church, and asked
Karen if she would go with them, but she looked sadly at
her crutches with tears in her eyes. So the others went to
hear the word of God, but she went into her little bedroom
alone. It was only big enough to hold a bed and a chair,
and she sat down here with her hymn book. As she was
devoutly reading it, the wind carried the sound of the organ
to her from the church, and she raised her face, wet with
tears, and said, "God help me!"

Then the sun shone clear and bright, and the angel of God stood before her in white robes, the same angel she had seen that fateful night at the church door. But he was no longer holding the sharp sword in his hand; instead, he held a beautiful green branch covered with roses. He touched the ceiling of the room with it, and the ceiling rose higher and higher, and a golden star shone where he had touched it. Then he touched the walls, and they opened out until she saw the organ being played, and the old pictures of pastors and their wives. There sat the congregation in their carved pews, singing from their hymn books.

The church itself had come to the poor girl in her narrow
little room — or else she had gone to the church. She was
sitting in a pew with the rest of the pastor's household, and
at the end of the hymn they looked up and nodded to her,
and said, "You were right to come, Karen!"
"It was the grace of God!" she replied.
And the organ played, and the choir of children's voices
rang out pure and sweet. Bright sunlight streamed warmly
in through the window and fell on the pew where Karen
was sitting. Her heart was so full of sunshine, peace, and
joy that it broke. Her soul flew up to God on the sunbeams,
and when she came before God's throne, no one asked her
about the red shoes.